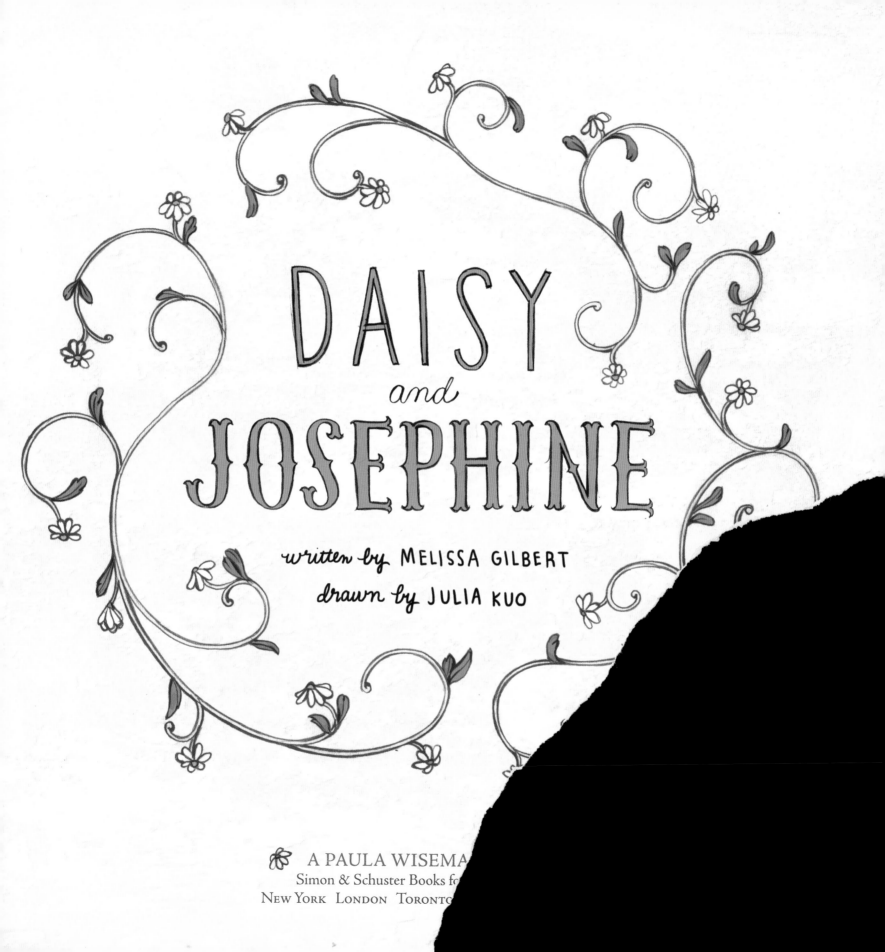

DAISY
and
JOSEPHINE

written by MELISSA GILBERT

drawn by JULIA KUO

A PAULA WISEMA...

Simon & Schuster Books fo...

NEW YORK LONDON TORONTO

For Daddy
—M. G.

For Spunky, my own little black dog
—J. K.

EADERS • An imprint of Simon & Schuster Children's Publishing Division • 1230 Avenue of the Americas, New York, New York
strations copyright © 2014 by Julia Kuo • All rights reserved, including the right of reproduction in whole or in part in any form.
demark of Simon & Schuster, Inc. • For information about special discounts for bulk purchases, please contact Simon & Schuster
ster.com. • The Simon & Schuster Speakers Bureau can bring authors to your live event. For more information or to book an
248-3049 or visit our website at www.simonspeakers.com. • Book design by Chloë Foglia • The text for this book is set in
olored digitally.

iner, and her teacher, Mrs. Minniear, but is lonely until her father brings home Josephine, a French

. 4. French bulldog—Fiction. 5. Dogs—Fiction.] • I. Kuo, Julia, illustrator. II. Title.

Daddy was Daisy's all-together favorite person. As far back as Daisy could remember, her daddy was there—making her pancakes, giving her tickles and squeezles.

Daddy was famous. People all over the world asked him to come sing, dance, and play music for them. But to Daisy he was just Daddy. "Daisy-doo, I love you from the top of your head to the tips of your toes and every freckle in between."

Daisy went everywhere Daddy went. And everywhere Daisy went, her teacher Mrs. Minniear went too.

Mrs. Minniear was kind and tall. She had pretty hands and smelled of roses. She taught Daisy all her lessons. When it was time to go on the road with Daddy, Mrs. Minniear packed up their schoolroom to go with them. New York! Miami! Las Vegas! There were lots of shows and new people to meet.

Even though Daisy loved her cozy family, she was lonely.
Sometimes she wished she had a friend to keep her company.

Every night at bedtime, Daisy would snuggle into her
daddy's arms and he'd sing Daisy her special song. Daisy
loved to listen to the sound of Daddy's big strong voice,
but she was too shy and too nervous to sing along.

"Daisy, Daisy, tell me your answer, do.
I'm half crazy over the love of you . . ."

One evening just before going on the road, Daisy heard a light knock on the door. *Tap, tap, tap.* "Daisy-doo. It's Daddy. I have a surprise for you." There was Daddy holding the funniest little creature Daisy had ever seen.

"Daisy, meet Josephine!"

"Oh, Daddy! Is it a cat? Is it a piglet?

What is it, Daddy?"

"None of the above, Daisy-doo. Josephine is a puppy," Daddy said. Josephine didn't look like any puppy Daisy had ever seen. She had no tail, giant ears, and a smooshy nose. Josephine's bottom teeth stuck out so far that Daisy could even see a bit of Josephine's teeny pink tongue peeking out.

"Why don't you two go play outside before it gets dark."

"Yes, Daddy," said Daisy.

Daisy tried to take Josephine down the back steps. But Josephine wouldn't budge. So Daisy scooped Josephine up in her arms and carried her.

"Don't go any farther than the backyard where I can see you,"
Mrs. Minniear called after Daisy as she walked out the door.

"Okay, let's play a game." Daisy grabbed the nicest stick she could find and tossed it.

"Fetch, Josephine!"

But Josephine would not fetch.

Josephine got comfy in a lawn chair instead.

"Look, Josephine!" said Daisy. "A squirrel. Let's chase it!"

But Josephine did not want to chase
a squirrel; she sniffed some flowers.

Daisy threw a bright, bouncy ball.

"Catch, Josephine!"

But Josephine did not want to catch the ball; she batted at a butterfly.

"You don't want to fetch. You don't want to chase.
You don't want to catch. What do you want to do?"
asked Daisy.

"Play dress-up!" said Josephine.

"Wait. . . . You can . . . talk?" asked Daisy.

"*Oui!* Can you speak French?"

Daisy shook her head no.

"Well, I will teach you. You see, I am a French bulldog so I can speak French. Would you have any clothes I might wear?" asked Josephine, very politely. "All of the great designers of clothes are French. And I just love clothes! Oh, please, won't you help me find something stylish to put on?" said Josephine.

"*Oui?*" said Daisy.

In her room, Daisy pulled out outfit after outfit. Plain shirts, plain pants, plain jeans. "There's this . . . and this . . . and these . . . and that."

"*Non, non, non, ma chère*," said Josephine. "Let's see what else we can find! Do you have anything sparkly?"

"How about this?" asked Daisy.

"Oh, yes!" said Josephine.

"And this?" asked Daisy.

"Most definitely!" said Josephine.

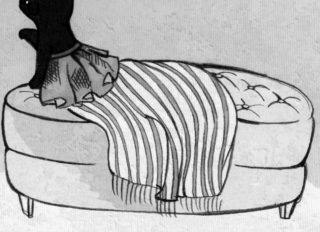

"What about these?" asked Daisy.

"*Oui!*" said Josephine.

"*Voilà!* Now, this is style! Let's find you some clothes that are *très chic.* That's French for 'very, very stylish.'"

"But Josephine . . . it's almost bedtime and I have to put on my jammies."

"Oh, Daisy, even pajamas can be stylish and fun!"

"Tadaaaaa!"

said Daisy.

"*Très bien!* Just one more thing. . . .

"*Voilà*. Hooray for the pajama princess!"

"Hooray for the pajamas *princesses*!" said Daisy.

Just then there was a knock on her door. *Tap, tap, tap.*

"Daisy-doo, are my girls ready for bed?"

"Oh, yes, Daddy," said Daisy as she threw her arms around Daddy's neck for a big squeezle.

Daddy picked Daisy and Josephine up in his arms and tucked them both in bed. Daisy snuggled close with Daddy and Josephine, and Daddy read them both a bedtime story and sang them a good-night song.

"I love you, my beautiful Daisy-doo."

"I love you too, Daddy."

"I love you, Josephine."

"*Je t'aime aussi*. I love you, too," whispered Josephine.

The room was still and oh so quiet.

"Daisy, will you sing me a lullaby?" asked Josephine.

Daisy took a deep breath and shyly, quietly, began to sing to her new friend.

"Josephine, Josephine, tell me your answer, do.
I'm half crazy over the love of you."